Rocky & Splash's First Lighthouse Dog Adventure

Dr. Tommy Dickey, Illustrated by A. Darling

Dedication

This book is dedicated to past and present members of the U.S. coastal lifesaving services which date back to 1790. These include the U.S. Revenue Cutter Service, the U.S. Life-Saving Service, and the U.S. Coast Guard. The book is also dedicated to both male and female lighthouse keepers, their families, and beloved dogs who helped to enrich life at lighthouses and contributed to saving many lives. The lighthouse dogs were clearly forerunners of today's therapy and emotional support dogs.

Acknowledgements

I would like to thank Terrie Strom, Derek Manov, David Dickey and Todd Dickey, who assisted in the writing of this book. Also, I appreciate the support of librarians and administrators of the many facilities and institutions who have welcomed our therapy dog visits. CJ Johnston and her daughters are thanked for their loving assistance with my Great Pyrenees therapy dogs for over a decade. Finally, I would like to thank Aran Darling for providing his insights, suggestions, and wonderful illustrations for this book, as well as Izzy de la Meme for support with coloring and layout.

Disclaimers

Names, characters, places, incidents, and events described and illustrated in this book are products of the author's imagination and are either fictitious or used in a fictitious manner. Opinions expressed in this manuscript are solely the author's. They do not represent the opinions or thoughts of the publisher. Mention of specific organizations in this book does not imply their endorsement of this book nor does their mention imply the organizations' endorsement by the publisher. The author warrants that he owns legal rights to publish all of the material in this book. No part of this book or its illustrations may be reproduced or transmitted in any form without permission in writing from the author except for inclusion of brief quotations in reviews.

© 2020, Dr. Tommy D. Dickey

Preface

My interest in writing began at age ten when my father, who was a sportswriter for a small-town newspaper in Indiana, helped me write a newspaper article on basketball. My first book was a college textbook entitled Exploring the World Ocean, and was co-authored with my good friend Sean Chamberlin. The second, The Therapy Dog Adventures of the Great Pyrenees Ted E. Bear and Friends, is a children's book based on decade-long therapy dog experiences with my Great Pyrenees dogs.

The present book builds on my interests in therapy and working dogs, lighthouses, and encouraging children to read. My Great Pyrenees therapy dogs, Teddy, Linkin, and Summer, have collectively done well over 3,000 visits and won over 60 awards. My interest in lighthouses began while I served in the U.S. Coast Guard before earning my Ph.D. in oceanography at Princeton University. As a professor at the University of Southern California and the University of California at Santa Barbara, I became interested in the historical period of the late 1800's and early 1900's because of my admiration for polar explorers. So, it is only natural that this book is set in this time period, which was also near the peak years of importance of lighthouses.

Foreword

This is the first in a series of lighthouse dog books for children. Its main characters are two dogs, a male Great Pyrenees dog named Rocky and a female Newfoundland dog named Splash, who are pressed into service as rescue dogs. They live at a lighthouse in Maine in 1900 with two children and their widow lighthouse keeper mom. The characters and events of the stories are fictitious, though loosely based on some actual lighthouse rescues of the late 1800's and early 1900's. The stories are told by Rocky, who is modeled after my Great Pyrenees named Linkin. Lighthouse keeper Minnie and her two children, 12-year old Becky and 10-year old Toby, are the primary human characters. The book is intended to encourage kids to read, to learn about an important period of American history, and to learn some life lessons through the actions of two dogs and their young caretakers. The book can be used in several different ways including: 1) pre-school and elementary school classroom and library reading, 2) therapy dog reading programs, and 3) a resource preparing for children's field trips to lighthouses. I hope that this book will be enjoyed by not only children, but also their teachers, relatives, and friends. Profits from this book will be donated to therapy dog organizations.

Hi! I am a Great Pyrenees dog named Rocky! I live at Cape Candy Cane Lighthouse in Maine in the year 1900. A lighthouse is usually a tall coastal or offshore tower with a bright signal light on top. Some have nearby buildings to live in. In 1900, almost 20,000 ships and boats transport goods and people on the ocean, lakes, rivers, and canals. At this time in history, we don't have cars, trucks, and airplanes yet! Over 800 lighthouses are being used to prevent shipwrecks and to save lives by marking hazardous locations and warning sailors of dangerous waterway conditions.

How did I become a lighthouse dog? Well, my friend Splash, a female Newfoundland puppy, and I were pets of the crew of a sailing ship named the *Lady Alice*. One stormy night, our ship broke apart and began to sink. Fortunately, a lighthouse keeper named Minnie and her children, 12-year old Becky, and 10-year old Toby, saw us in the stormy waters. Minnie rowed a boat out to our sinking ship and got us all safely to shore.

Captain James of the *Lady Alice*, the crew, Splash, and I were cold, wet, and scared during Minnie's heroic rescue. Once inside the lighthouse, Becky and Toby dried Splash and me and cuddled us near a nice warm fireplace. They also gave us some biscuits to eat. Minnie took care of the crew and gave them some blankets and warm food and drinks.

After a few days, the local mailboat with Captain Von came to Cape Candy Cane Lighthouse to take the Lady Alice's captain and crew, Splash, and me to a port city down the coast. Before boarding, Captain James said, "Minnie, Becky, and Toby, in appreciation for saving our lives, the crew and I want you to have a couple of presents from us – Rocky and Splash!" Splash and I were sooooooo happy, as we had already fallen in love with the family.

Lighthouses come in many different sizes, shapes, and colors. Our lighthouse has a special candy cane striped "daymark" so ships at sea know that they are seeing our lighthouse at Cape Candy Cane. The light can be seen for about 20 miles at sea on clear nights. It has a special flashing light signal so sailors can identify it. On foggy days and nights, a bell is rung to help sailors locate the lighthouse. Splash and I have even learned how to ring the bell! Everyone works at a lighthouse – even the dogs!

One day, Becky asked her Mom why Splash has web-like paws and then Toby noticed that I have extra claws on my back feet. Minnie had read about Newfoundland and Great Pyrenees dogs. She said, "Newfies, with webbed feet, are water dogs and well-adapted to be great swimmers and even water life-saving dogs. On the other hand, Great Pyrenees are mountain dogs and have extra back claws that some people think help them climb rocks and cliffs."

One sunny day, Splash and I decided to dig a hole on a hill near the lighthouse. Becky and Toby came by and noticed that we had uncovered a box. Becky exclaimed, "This is a time capsule box that was placed in the ground when the lighthouse was built 50 years ago! I just read about this in a very old logbook entry for our lighthouse." The time capsule box was filled with objects typical of the year 1850.

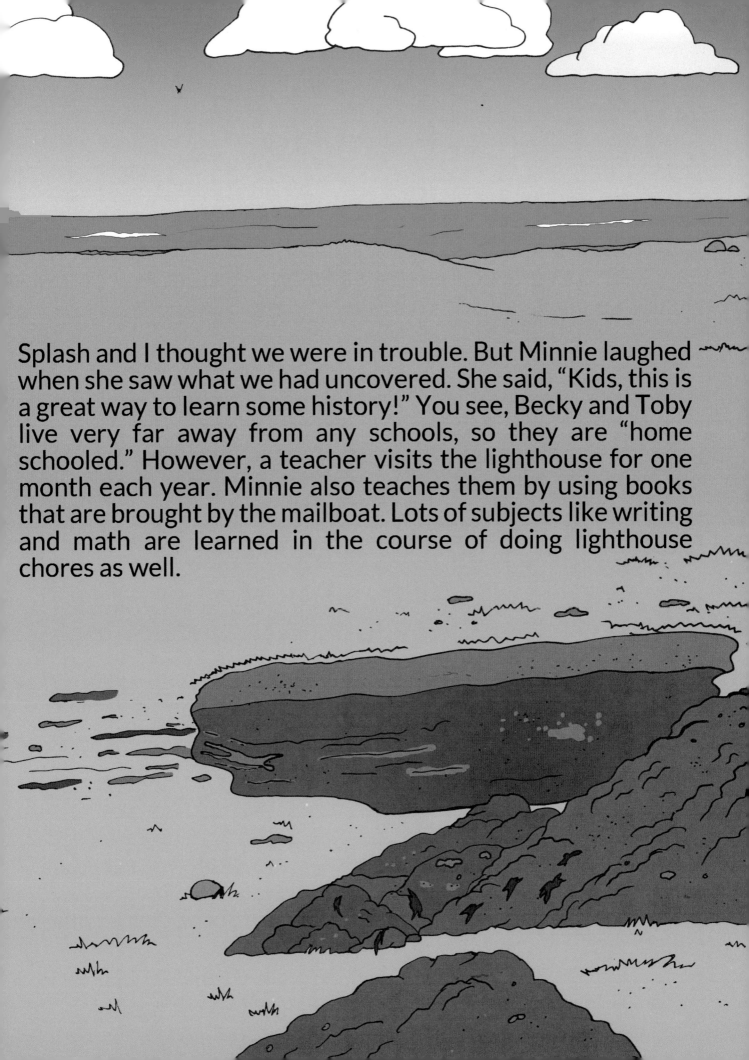

Splash and I thought we were in trouble. But Minnie laughed when she saw what we had uncovered. She said, "Kids, this is a great way to learn some history!" You see, Becky and Toby live very far away from any schools, so they are "home schooled." However, a teacher visits the lighthouse for one month each year. Minnie also teaches them by using books that are brought by the mailboat. Lots of subjects like writing and math are learned in the course of doing lighthouse chores as well.

Minnie told us, "Our lighthouse was built 50 years ago." She said, "These paintings show how steam engines are beginning to be used to propel ships." I saw a ball in the box and ran around with it! It was something called a baseball used for a funny game first played in 1846. We next found a newspaper with the headline 'Gold!! Gold!!' Minnie explained that 300,000 people had moved to California to find gold in 1849.

There is no electricity, telephone, radio, or computer at our 1900 lighthouse. So, what do we do here at the lighthouse? Becky and Toby read lots of books and play card and board games. They do lighthouse chores like cleaning the lighthouse lens and windows dirtied by lighthouse lamp smoke. They carry lamp fuel up the 50 steps of the lighthouse and help Minnie write notes in the lighthouse logbook. The logbook is used to record everything that happens at the lighthouse. They also watch for ships in distress. They are really junior lighthouse keepers.

One afternoon, Toby decided to take the lighthouse rowboat offshore without asking Minnie. Becky was wondering where Toby might be as she took Splash and me for a walk along the shore. Then, she heard some screams out on the water. It was Toby! He had drifted in the boat way off shore as the winds had shifted with an approaching storm. Also, the tide was going out. Off the Maine coast, the tides are very high creating fast currents. Becky yelled out to Toby, "We'll save you!" She exclaimed, "Rocky and Splash, we have to save Toby!"

Becky remembered that there was a rope with a knotted ball called a 'monkey fist' up on the steep and rocky cliff. She said, "Rocky, run up the cliff and bring me the 'monkey fist' rope as fast as you can. I scampered up the cliff using my extra back claws to advantage. When I returned, Becky said, "Splash, now you have to swim as fast as you can with those big webbed paws and give the 'monkey fist' rope to Toby."

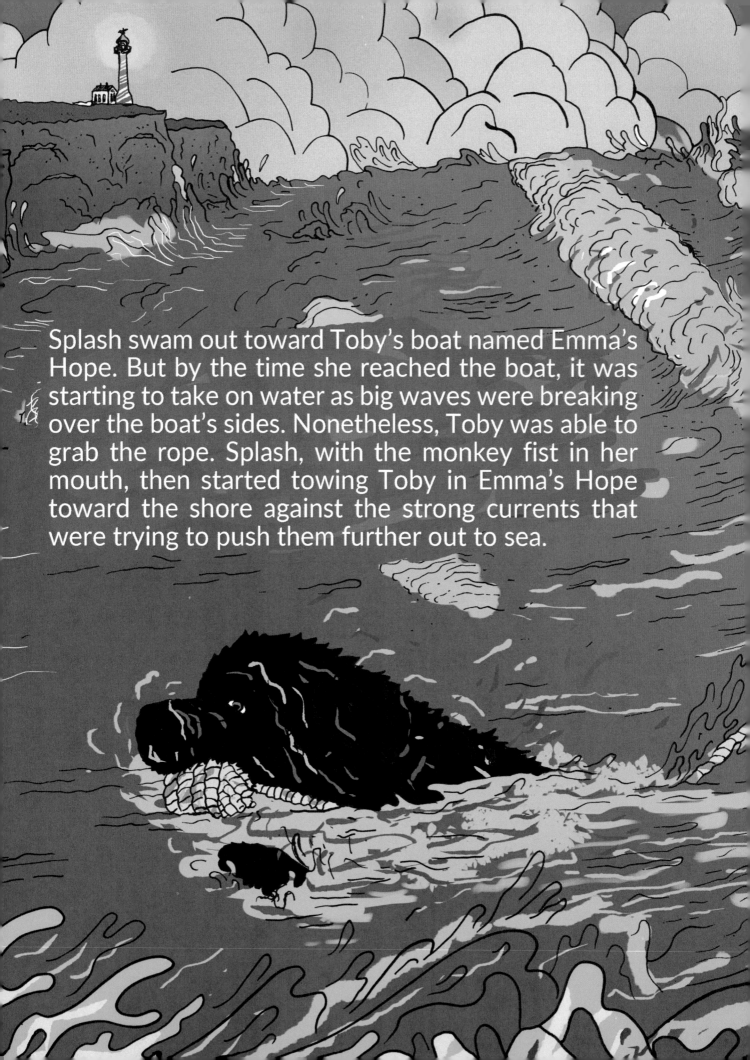

Splash swam out toward Toby's boat named Emma's Hope. But by the time she reached the boat, it was starting to take on water as big waves were breaking over the boat's sides. Nonetheless, Toby was able to grab the rope. Splash, with the monkey fist in her mouth, then started towing Toby in Emma's Hope toward the shore against the strong currents that were trying to push them further out to sea.

Toby and Splash slowly approached the shore as Becky and I nervously watched. Toby and Splash were very tired and out of breath as they reached shore. Toby and Becky hugged each other and then Splash and me. Toby thanked Becky, Splash, and me. He then said, "I bet I am in big trouble with Mom!"

We walked to the lighthouse and told Minnie what had happened. Minnie patiently asked, "Toby, what have you learned?" He replied, "Never go out on the water by myself and ask permission first." Then Minnie asked, "Becky, what have you learned?" Becky replied, "Learn as much as I can. Like which kind of dog is best suited for a task! Rocky for rock climbing and Splash for swimming!" Finally, Minnie said, "I need a big hug from our heroic dogs! I'll never forget this day! Rocky and Splash, you are the best presents Candy Cane Lighthouse has ever received!"

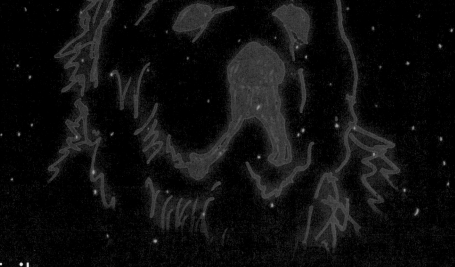

Epilogue

Hundreds of women served as lighthouse keepers according to the books Women Who Kept the Lights and Mind the Light, Katie, both written by Mary Louise Clifford and J. Candace Clifford. Often, women, by necessity, took over lighthouse keeping duties following the injury or loss of their lighthouse keeper husbands.

The Cliffords state that 144 women were officially appointed lighthouse keepers in the U.S. between 1845 and 1912 and over twice as many women served as assistant lighthouse keepers. Many others served as lighthouse keepers without official titles. Often, these women were raising children who had lighthouse dog companions. The Cliffords' books are highly recommended for those wishing to learn more about heroic women lighthouse keepers.

Afterword

After writing this book, the author discovered that there is a real-life candy cane striped lighthouse in Lake Michigan. This lighthouse, White Shoal Light, has been depicted on Michigan car license plates to raise funds to save Michigan lighthouses. There are about 150 lighthouses on the Great Lakes with over 50 on Lake Michigan alone. Maine has 80 lighthouses with a coastline length of about 3,500 miles or over 5,000 miles counting its islands' coastlines.

There are several U.S. organizations such as the Michigan Lighthouse Conservancy (see http://www.michiganlights.com/) and the U.S. Lighthouse Society (see https://uslhs.org/) working hard to save and preserve lighthouses. Lighthouse Digest Magazine is recommended as an excellent publication providing historical information about lighthouses and their preservation (see http://www.lighthousedigest.com/).